DATE DUE

CATCH THAT CAT!

CATCH THAT CAT!

Fernando Krahn

E. P. DUTTON • NEW YORK

Library of Congress Cataloging in Publication Data

Krahn, Fernando.   Catch that cat!

SUMMARY: The adventures of a little boy chasing
his runaway cat.
[1. Stories without words]   I. Title.
PZ7.K8585Cat   [E]   77-20820   ISBN: 0-525-27555-X

Published in the United States by E. P. Dutton, a Division
of Sequoia-Elsevier Publishing Company, Inc., New York

Published simultaneously in Canada by Clarke,
Irwin & Company Limited, Toronto and Vancouver

Editor: Ann Troy   Designer: Jennifer Dossin
Printed in the U.S.A.   First Edition
10 9 8 7 6 5 4 3 2 1